BLUBBER BOILER

CROOKJAW

by Caron Lee Cohen

pictures by Linda Bronson

Henry Holt and Company ～ New York

For Eva Lewis, my dear mother
—C. L. C.

For David Porter and his family
—L. B.

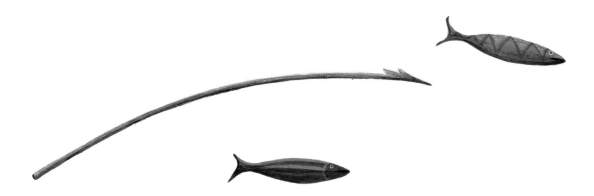

Henry Holt and Company, Inc., *Publishers since 1866*
115 West 18th Street, New York, New York 10011

Henry Holt is a registered trademark of Henry Holt and Company, Inc.
Text copyright © 1997 by Caron Lee Cohen. Illustrations copyright © 1997 by Linda Bronson
All rights reserved.
Published in Canada by Fitzhenry & Whiteside Ltd., 195 Allstate Parkway, Markham, Ontario L3R 4T8.
Library of Congress Cataloging-in-Publication Data
Crookjaw / by Caron Lee Cohen; pictures by Linda Bronson.
Summary: In this folktale from New England, a fisherman climbs into the mouth of
an infamous whale named Crookjaw and discovers a surprise in her gullet.
[1. Folklore—New England.] I. Bronson, Linda, ill. II. Title.
PZ7.C65974Co 1997 398.2—dc21 [E] 96-44214
ISBN 0-8050-5300-X / First Edition—1997
Typography by Martha Rago
The artist used oil paints on board to create the illustrations for this book.
Printed in the United States of America on acid-free paper. ∞
1 3 5 7 9 10 8 6 4 2

In the mid-1600s the New England colonists began whaling. For the next two hundred years seafarers set out from bustling ports — Nantucket, Martha's Vineyard, and New Bedford, Massachusetts — to harpoon whales and boil their blubber for the precious whale oil that was sold around the world to light oil lamps.

But whaling was dangerous. There were treacherous storms at sea. Whales — the largest creatures on earth—could be monsters of destruction, smashing ships, drowning seamen. Fears abounded. Superstitions grew. Witches with grudges against sailors or sea captains were frequently blamed for ocean tragedies. Some witches were thought to reside in whales' bellies, causing havoc far out at sea. But where there were witches, there were remedies to ward them off. In colonial New England, everyone knew that silver was the one metal that could pierce a witch's skin, destroying her and putting an end to all her spells.

While whaling was dangerous for seafarers, it was even more dangerous for whales. American whaling virtually ended in the late 1800s, but the industry increased in other parts of the world. The United States has strongly opposed whaling in recent years, and has joined other nations to ban the killing. Fortunately, the slaughter has been dramatically reduced. All whale species are currently safe from extinction, but they will need protection for many years to reach their earlier numbers.

The folklore of New England abounds with tales of witches, seafarers, and the sea. In this version of Crookjaw, I have included another bit of local lore — red shoes — a dead give-away that the wearer is a witch.

The day Ichabod Paddock was born, he took his pappy's harpoon for a teething ring. That afternoon he dove into Nantucket Sound. He swam, slick as an eel in a barrel of jellyfish. He swung his teething ring and caught his first killer whale.

By the time he was ten, he'd caught 431 whales from his boat, the *Blubber Boiler*. He got so famous, folks all over New England were naming their dogs, horses, kids, and whaleboats after him. The Boston Navy Yard moved Noah's picture over and made Ichabod number one in the Seafarers' Hall of Fame.

But his wife, Smilinda, was his biggest fan. "A savage whale can seethe and spit, jump and smash," she'd say. "But my Ichabod will get 'er every time."

And it was true. Until one day when Ichabod met Crookjaw in
the Atlantic Ocean. The captain saw something huge breaking
water and spouting. "Thar she blows!" he hollered.

Then he heard her shrill calls and low moans. And he caught sight of her crooked jaws. That whale seethed, and she spit. She jumped, and she smashed.

The captain let fly harpoon after harpoon. But the whale always got away. Day in and day out the *Blubber Boiler* chased Crookjaw. Day in and day out Crookjaw ranted and raved, crashed and splashed. Time and again she nearly wrecked that boat.

One morning the whale changed. There was no more racing up and down. She just lolled around acting cute. Ichabod let fly, but his harpoon just bounced off that sea devil. "Sure as eggs is eggs, that whale is spellbound!" said the captain.

Then Ichabod heard a strange howl——*Awooooooo, awooooooo, shshshshshshsh, awooooooo*——calling him. He jumped overboard. Dove into that whale's crooked jaws and swam down her gullet.

He came to a room with a kettle of fish on the floor. And a table spread with Cape Cod cranberry sauce, corn bread, turkey pot pie, apples and pears, yams and carrots, succotash and Indian pudding, and his very favorite——Boston baked beans for dessert.

And there was a lady. All dressed up in a frilly frock. Walking around in that whale's belly wearing red shoes. Tucked in her belt was a deck of cards. She was singing the most beautiful song he'd ever heard:

Ichabod, Ichabod, awooooomi, wooooooo,
Awooooooo, awooooooo, shshshshshshsh, awooooooo.

Then she spoke to him:

Omi, nomi, pori, wooooooo.
Nomi, pori, omi, yooooooo.
Ishy, wishy, fishy, wishshshshshshsh.
Ina, fishy, isa, witchchchchchchch.

"Glory be! A language of fishes," said the captain. "What a surprise, finding the likes o' you in here!"

"I always do my traveling by whale," she said. "And my shipwrecking, too. I wreck 'em smash-bang on the spot. Or bit by bit while I work their captains to death."

But it didn't matter what she said. Ichabod was bewitched. They sat down for supper. He ate cooked vittles. She ate live barracuda from the kettle. Then the two of them played Go Fish.

"You're awful good at Go Fish," the lady said the next morning.
"And that's what you're gonna do for me. Now *go fish!* Net me some
barracuda."

She sent him back out to the *Blubber Boiler* with hot barnacle stew.
After eating it all up, the crew was bewitched, too.

Every day Ichabod and the crew netted barracuda. Every night Ichabod
dove into the whale's jaws with a full net. It was the same thing day in
and day out.

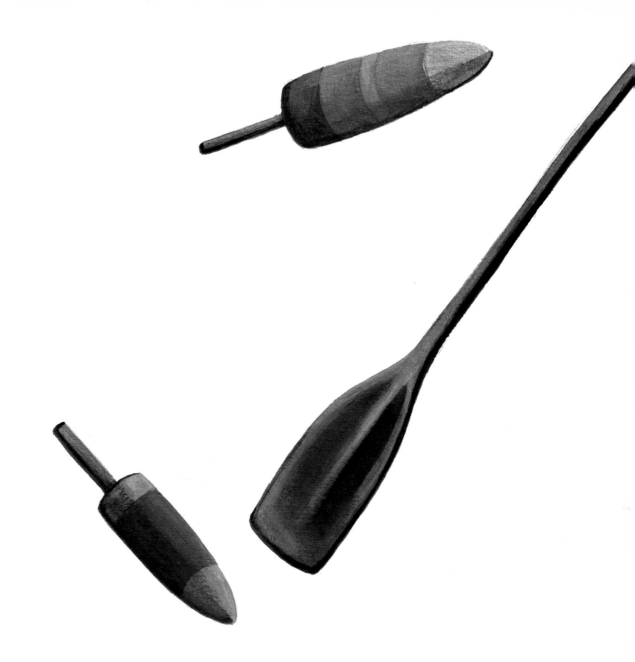

Now on Nantucket Island, Smilinda was waiting day in and day out. Every day she kept her chin up. But every night she had the worst nightmare — Ichabod getting chewed in the jaws of some savage sea devil. She couldn't let another day go in and out. So she hopped into a little rowboat and rowed out to sea.

By and by, she spotted two feet on their way into a whale's mouth. Those feet were wearing the very boots she'd given Ichabod on their wedding day. "That's my Ichabod!" she cried.

Then she heard a howl: *Awooooooo, awooooooo,*

shshshshshshsh, awoooooooo. And she saw the crew sleepwalking
on the half-wrecked *Blubber Boiler*. And the whale just sashaying
around. Smilinda knew what was ailing them. She rowed back to
Nantucket and got to work.

She took her grandma's set of silver egg cups from the kitchen cupboard. She melted and shaped, melted and shaped that silver till she had a harpoon.

Then she rowed out to sea. When Smilinda spotted the captain dog-paddling in the water, she rowed on up. Ichabod didn't look good. He looked half-chewed, half-dead, and all wet.

"My Ichabod!" she said. "That ain't no way to keep your britches dry. Git aloft."

"Jumpin' tadpoles! It's Smilinda." Ichabod climbed into the little rowboat.

"Lookie here," she said, "I brought this shiny new harpoon for you, darlin'."

He looked at it as if he'd never seen one before. Then he flung that hook. And gosh-a'-mighty! It stuck right into Crookjaw.

That sea devil roared louder than an ocean volcano showing off. She raced faster than a tidal wave in a hurry. Crookjaw dragged that rowboat clear up and down the entire Atlantic Ocean.

The whale finally got tired. She stopped to yawn only a yard from the *Blubber Boiler*. And jumpin' codfish! A big piece of deadwood floated out of that whale's crooked jaws, all dressed up in a frilly frock. Out floated a deck of cards. And one red shoe.

All the spells were over.

Ichabod was so out-and-out flabbergasted, he dropped the harpoon rope. Only whale he ever let get away! Crookjaw slapped her tail on the water and swam off.

Smilinda didn't tell Ichabod the shiny new harpoon was made of pure silver. That's the one metal that turns a witch to wood. And Ichabod didn't ask what happened to grandma's silver egg cups.

But from then on, Ichabod Paddock never met another bewitched whale. And search as he might out at sea, he never found the other red shoe.

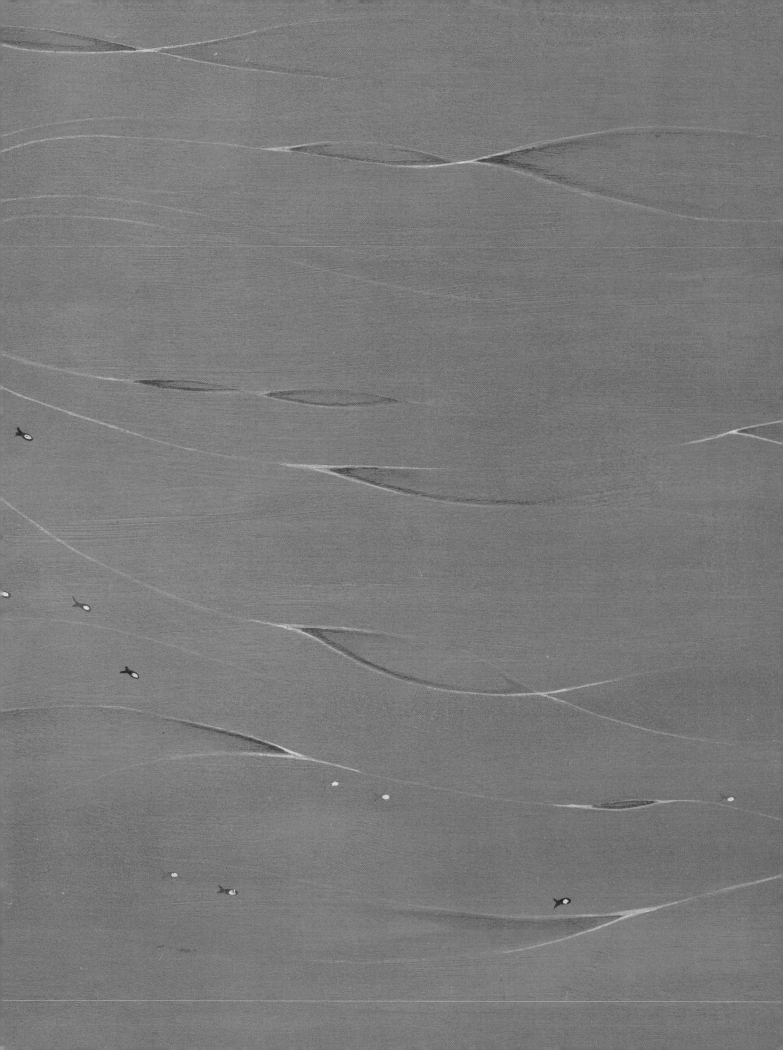